How the Gecko Lost his Tail

by Bruce Hale

Based on his book,
The Adventures of Space Gecko

WORDS + PICTURES
PUBLISHING, INC

This book is dedicated to my wife, Janette.

Also by Bruce Hale:

Legend of the Laughing Gecko
Surf Gecko to the Rescue!
Moki and the Magic Surfboard
Moki the Gecko's Best Christmas Ever

Library of Congress Catalog Card Number: 99-072863
ISBN: 0-9621280-8-2

Printed in China.

First printing, October 1999
Second printing, June 2002
Third printing, September 2008

O ne hot island day, Moki the Gecko argued with
his parents because they wouldn't get him a new surfboard. "You're so mean!" he shouted, and stomped
down to the beach to cool off. But when he returned,
something was different. Something was wrong.

He looked all around. Nobody home. Moki went to
the other animals asking, "Have you seen my parents?"

But nobody had. The little gecko dragged home
alone.

Outside the door sat his friend, Pueo the owl.

"Pueo, I can't find my parents," sighed Moki. "I don't know what to do."

The owl shifted slowly from foot to foot. "You're not going to like this," he said. "'Io the Hawk saw the whole thing."

Moki braced himself: "What?"

Pueo continued, "Your parents were upset. They went walking on the side of the island where nobody goes, by the lake where Moon takes her bath. They got careless. Your parents fell in the moon water."

"No!" said Moki. He knew that if you touched moon water, you could go crazy, or even worse, you could be captured by the moon. Were his parents so upset they forgot this?

"Moon took them up into the sky," the owl said softly. "They're gone, Moki."

Moki flopped down and cried from his heart. Pueo brushed velvety wingfeathers over his friend's shoulders. "Oh, Moki, don't worry — we'll think of something," he said. "Come on, let's go see 'Io the Hawk. Maybe she can tell us more."

Moki and Pueo found the hawk perched on the old ironwood tree.

"Hmph," she sniffed. "I've told you all.
Your careless parents took the fall,
and now you want to bring them back?
All I can say is, 'good luck, Jack.'"
'Io returned to grooming her
bright feathers.

"But 'Io, I must go help them,"
Moki replied. "Please, can you
fly me to the moon?"

The hawk looked icicles at
Moki with her golden eyes.
"Why should I try?"
she asked him. "See,
what have you ever done
for me?
You interrupt me
with your woe.
I've told you all I can,
now go!"

Moki slumped away. "Aw, don't worry," said Pueo. "She's just sore because she knows she can't fly as high as the moon. No bird can."

"But how will I ever get to my parents?" asked the little gecko. Pueo scratched his head. "There's one last chance, but it could be dangerous," he said. "Go ask the great volcano. If she doesn't burn you up, she just might help you. Good luck."

By the time Moki reached
the volcano, the afternoon
sun hung low. He took a deep
breath and started climbing.
Up he went, higher and higher.
Clouds brushed his face like the
fingers of ghosts, but still he
climbed on.

Once Moki slipped and hung
by his tail over a long drop. He
grabbed for a rock, but it fell off the
cliff. Would Moki follow? No -- his
sticky gecko feet helped get him back
on the trail.

Finally, he stood at the top. Hot steam poured from the mouth of the crater as he tiptoed nearer. Moki kneeled.

"Great Volcano, I bring an offering," he said, placing a special plant gently on the rock. "My parents fell in moon water and Moon took them away. Please help me save them."

The volcano hissed softly, "Why? They made their mistake. What's done is done."

"But it's my fault," said Moki. "I made them so angry, they got careless. Besides, I love them. I can't just let them go without doing something."

The volcano steamed in silence. "You want my help? Very well," she said at last. "Come closer." Moki walked to the jagged edge of the crater. The heat made him sweat like a waterfall.

"Ready?" asked the volcano. "Y-y-yes, your volcano-ship," said Moki. "Then jump," commanded the fiery goddess. Moki just stood there. Only a crazy gecko would jump into red-hot lava.

"Why do you wait? Do you want my help or not?" rumbled the volcano. Her lava bubbled angrily. "Jump!" she boomed. Moki took two steps back, hopped and jumped.....

......into the heart of the crater.

FAVOOOMM! A huge blast of steam shot out of the volcano's mouth, sweeping Moki ahead of it, up into the night sky. Faster and faster he flew, past the highest clouds, away from the familiar Earth and into space itself. Moki shut his eyes tightly.

When he opened them again, he found himself drifting in a cool sea of midnight blue. Stars sparkled bright above and below him. The sky glowed and pulsed. Then Moki turned around.

Looming near in the night sky, filling his sight like a huge silver ball, was the moon. So beautiful, so big — she took his breath away. As Moki drifted closer, he thought he could see a woman's face behind the silver light.

Moon smiled, "Hello, little one, what are you doing so far from home?"

"It's about my parents," said Moki. "Please. They didn't mean to touch your water, I'd like them to come home now."

Moon's smile faded. "Ah, your mother and father," she said. "Too late. They fell in my lake, and now they're mine."

"Please," said Moki. "Can't I do something to change your mind?"

"There is something," said Moon, "but I doubt you can do it. The jealous Sun has stolen my mirror, and I cannot look upon my face. You are small and clever.

"Bring me the mirror and I will free your parents."

"But how do I get it?" asked Moki.

"That's your problem," said Moon. Just then, a friendly asteroid -- or space boulder -- the size of a small dog drifted towards Moki.

"Can you help me?" he asked the asteroid. It bobbed up and down eagerly. "Thank you. I think I'll call you Simon, if you don't mind."

The friendly space boulder nodded again.

Moki sat in one of the asteroid's small
craters and hung on tightly as the little space
boulder picked up speed. Soon, they rounded
the Earth and saw it ahead, blinding and glorious in
the sky — the Sun.

Here goes nothing, thought Moki. If I fail, I'll
probably end up as Roast Gecko Au Gratin.
    As he drew nearer, Moki could hardly see, for the
bright light. He scrunched down lower, trying to hide.
But it was no use.

"Who's there?" called Sun. "Who comes to see me in all my splendor?"

"Moki, a small gecko from Earth," said Moki, sitting up.

"Don't you think I'm beautiful?" said Sun. "No star in the universe has rays as glorious as mine. I'm a superstar, I am."

Moon is prettier, thought Moki. But of course, he didn't say that. Instead, he asked, "How do you know you're so beautiful? Have you ever seen yourself?"

"What?! Foolish earth creature!" bellowed the sun. "Everyone knows I'm hot stuff. But it's true I haven't seen myself. That's why I got this." He held up a small mirror.

"Great Sun, you cannot see your whole body," Moki said. "Better throw me the mirror, so I can show you." Now the sun was bright, but he wasn't too bright, you see. He tossed the mirror to Moki, who let Simon the asteroid drift a little further away. "How's this?" asked the gecko, holding up the mirror.

If you've ever tried to look at the sun, you know how it can hurt your eyes. But the Sun didn't know that. Blinded by his own light, he howled like a mad dog. Moki saw his chance.

"Go, Simon!" he shouted, and VAZZOOSH! -- the asteroid zipped away from the Sun like a stone from a slingshot.

"Come back here!" bellowed the Sun. His mighty rays shot out as Moki tried to shrink down into a crater. Too late! Fingers of flame burned Moki's tail. "Yow!" cried the gecko.

In another two shakes, the little asteroid flew beyond the sun's reach. Moki's poor tail was black, burnt and oh, so painful. It hurt worse than a thousand sunburns.

"I hope Sun learned his lesson," he told Simon. "I sure learned mine -- don't bug a superstar, or you might get burned."

Soon the asteroid brought him back to the moon.
Moon smiled hopefully, "Well? What luck?"
Moki managed to stand up. "I got your mirror," he
said. "Now give me back my parents."

Moon's smile melted like snow. "Not so fast," she said. "Maybe I have another task for you before I'll let them go."

Moki's shoulders sagged. Then, he slowly straightened and held up the mirror. "Maybe I'll take this back to Earth with me and neither one of us will get what we want," he said.

Moon sighed, "Oh, well. It was worth a try. Here, take my magic silver cup and pour this on your tail."

Moki poured the shining water on his blackened stump of a tail and — miracle of miracles — he grew back a brand new tail, strong and shiny and green. He tossed the mirror to the moon.

"I grant you a special gift," said Moon. "From now on, all geckos can grow back their tails as you have done. Now go around to my dark side where you will find your mother and father. Take them and return home, with my blessing."

Sure enough, on the Moon's dark side, Moki found his parents. They were having a party with some strange-looking space aliens.

The three geckos greeted each other with laughter and tears and "Oh-how-I-missed-you." Then, "I've come to take you home," said Moki.

"That's very brave of you to come this far," said his mother, "but we don't want to go."

"What?!" Moki the Gecko couldn't believe his ears.

"That's right," his father said. "We like it here with our new friends. Stay with us and become a moon gecko."

Moki looked up in the sky to see the Earth, floating like a blue-green ball. He looked at the moon — no waves, no trees. Then he searched his heart.

"Our home is back there," he said finally, "with the ocean and forest and volcano. Come back with me. The moon is no place for a gecko to be."

Moki's parents looked at each other, then at their new friends.

"Well, I suppose we could always come back to visit," said his mother.

"Absolutely," said Moki. "Just do me a favor: Stay away from that moon water."

Moki's parents laughed and hugged their son. The three geckos climbed aboard the little asteroid.

"Home, Simon!" cried Moki.

And Simon took off.

Simon the space boulder danced through the midnight blue sky, moving faster and faster as it neared the Earth. The gecko family hung on tight.

Before long, they pierced the atmosphere and ripped down through the clouds.

Finally, they landed — KERBLUNK! — right in the ocean off Moki's beach. A gentle wave rolled the asteroid up the sand, tumbling the geckos in the surf. They were home at last.

Moki's father ran to tell all the geckos about the moon's blessing.

   "And now, if you're ever cornered by cats, you can drop your tail to distract them," he said. "Then you can grow it back again, thanks to the Moon and Moki."

   The geckos cheered.

   "Son, I'm so proud of you," said Moki's mother.

   "Thanks, Mom and Dad," said Moki. He grinned. "Now, about that new surfboard..."